KINGSTON UPON HULL CITY LIBRARIES		
B37274008 6		
Peters Books	15-Jan-02	
		£8.99
SCHOOLS		HCS

© Aladdin Books Ltd 2001

Designed and produced by
Aladdin Books Ltd
28 Percy Street
London W1P 0LD

First published in
Great Britain in 2001 by
Franklin Watts
96 Leonard Street
London EC2A 4XD

ISBN 0 7496 4123 1

A catalogue record for this book is available from the British Library.

Printed in Belgium
All rights reserved

Editor
Bibby Whittaker

Literacy Consultant
Jackie Holderness
Westminster Institute of Education,
Oxford Brookes University

Design
Flick, Book Design and Graphics

Picture Research
Brian Hunter Smart

Illustration
Mary Lonsdale for SGA

Picture Credits
Abbreviations: t – top, m – middle,
b – bottom, r – right, l – left,
c – centre. All photographs supplied by Select Pictures except for: Cover, 10tl, 17, 20-21, 23br — Corbis. 3, 4-5, 6tl, 18-19, 20tl, 22tr, 22bl, 24tr, 24ml — Digital Stock. 4tl, 8tl, 22tl — John Foxx Images. 9 — Danny Lehman/CORBIS. 12tl, 23ml — Stockbyte. 15 — Wolfgang Kaehler/CORBIS. 18tl — CORBIS.

READING ABOUT

Slow and Fast

By Jim Pipe

Aladdin/Watts
London • Sydney

Fast

What goes fast?

The car goes fast along the road. Kate and Dan are going to the fun park. They cannot wait to get there.

This big cat is fast, too.

It is called a cheetah.

It runs as fast as a car!

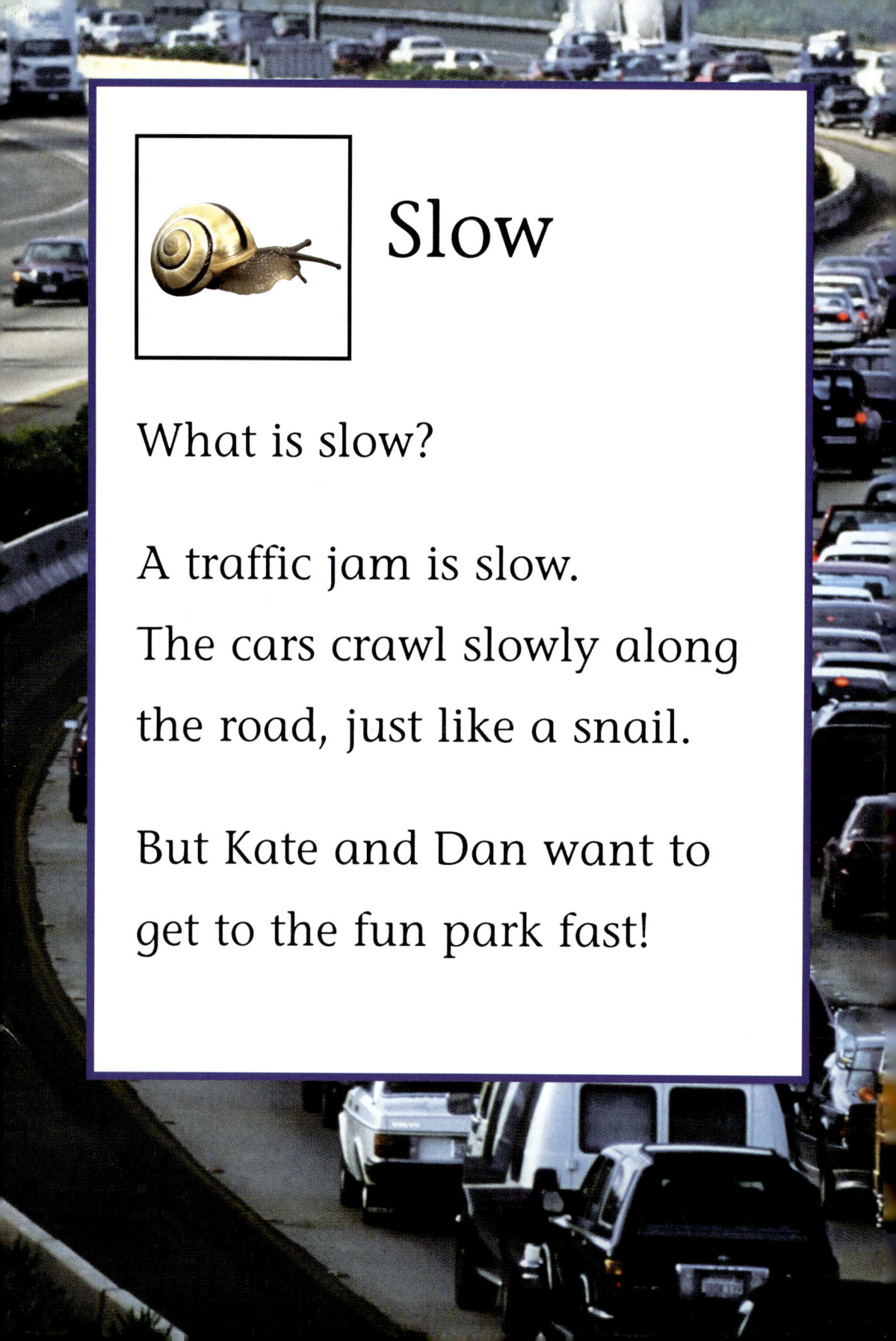

Slow

What is slow?

A traffic jam is slow. The cars crawl slowly along the road, just like a snail.

But Kate and Dan want to get to the fun park fast!

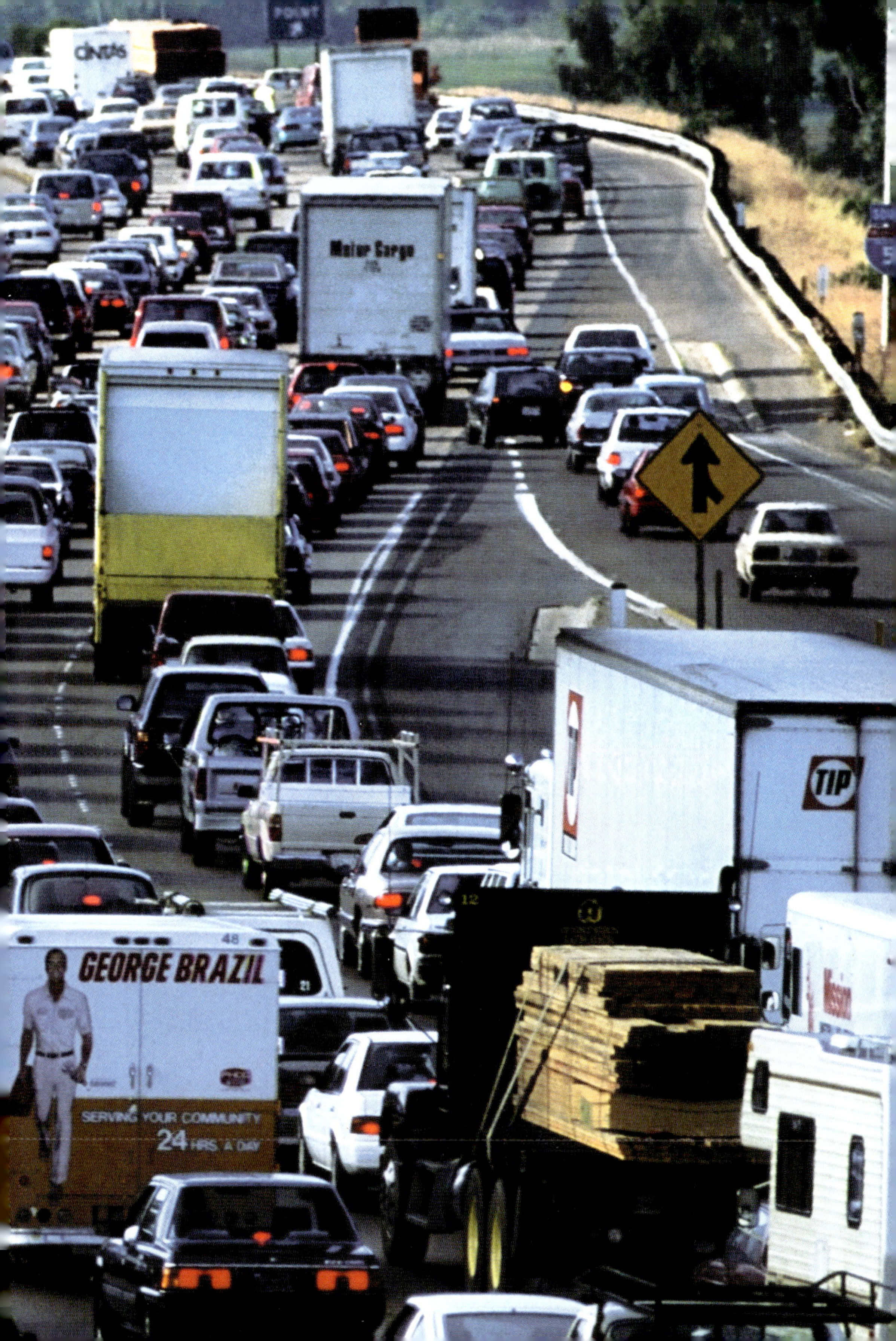
GEORGE BRAZIL
SERVING YOUR COMMUNITY
24 HRS. A DAY
TIP

Faster

Kate and Dan arrive at the park. They run to the slides.

Kate runs faster than Dan. But Dan is faster than Mum's friend Julie.

Who is faster on the slide?

Dan sits on a mat.

He slides faster than Kate.

He gets to the bottom first.

Slower

Who is slower?

Dan is slower. Kate says he is as slow as a tortoise. But when Kate runs too fast, she falls over.

Sometimes slower is better.

The man on the rope is slow.

If he goes too fast, he will fall off!

Faster and slower

What speeds up?

This ride speeds up!
It goes faster and faster.

Then the ride slows down.

It goes slower and slower.

When it stops, Dan and Kate get off.

Fastest

Kate and Dan watch the go-karts.

The go-karts go fast.

Mum's kart is the fastest.

It goes like a rocket!

Racing cars are very fast.

They race each other.

The fastest car wins the race.

Slowest

Who is the slowest?

Julie is. She takes a very long time to eat her pizza!

A sloth is one of the slowest animals. It can take all day to move along one branch.

Spinning

What spins fast?

The seats in this ride spin fast. They go round and round like a top. Dan and Kate get dizzy!

Kate and Dan like to spin fast.

Mum likes the big wheel.

It goes round very slowly.

Falling

Then Kate and Dan watch the air show.

A sky diver jumps from a plane. He falls faster and faster.

When the parachute opens, the sky diver slows down.

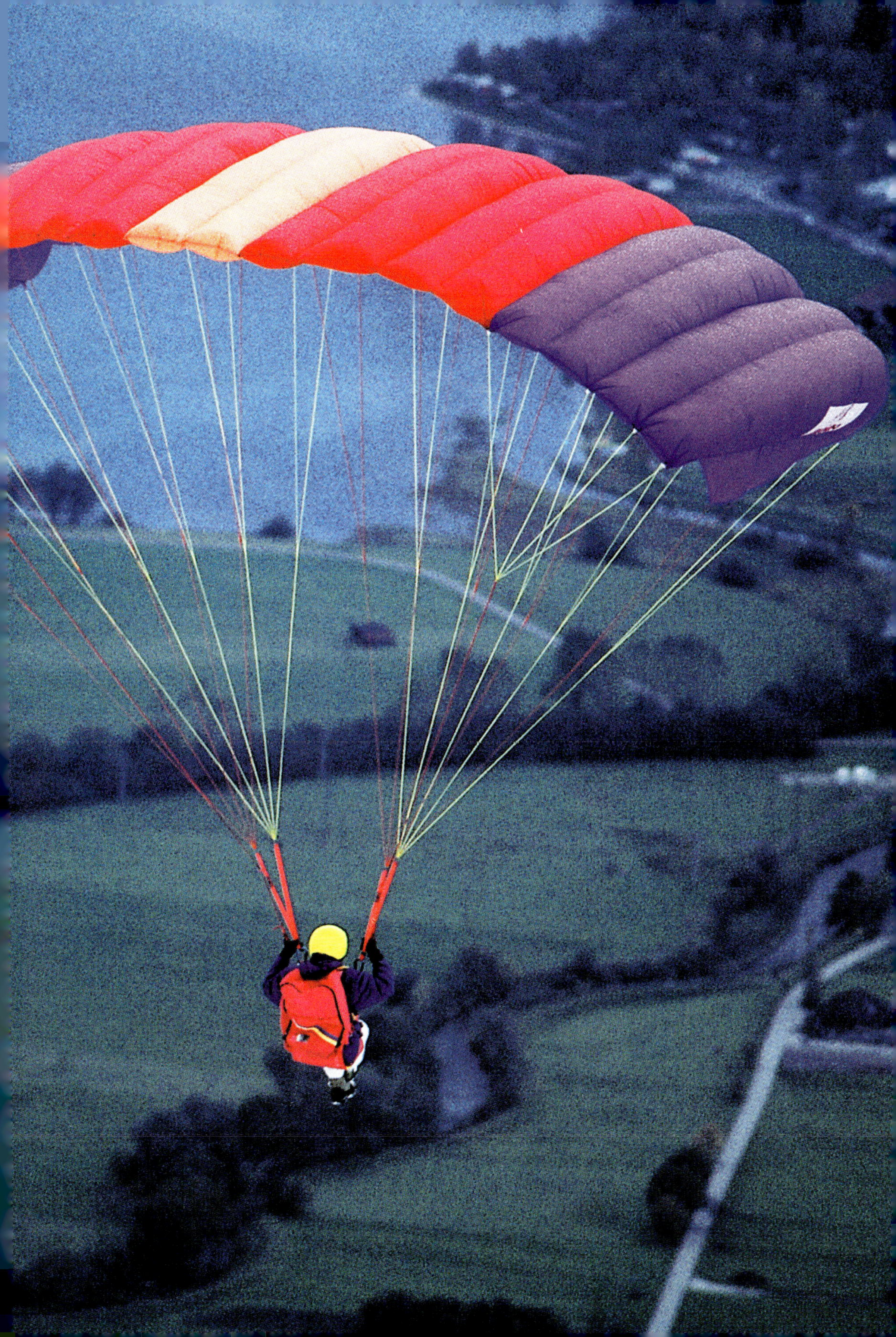

Slow and fast

What is slow and fast?

A rollercoaster goes slowly up the hill. But it comes down fast!

Everybody screams!

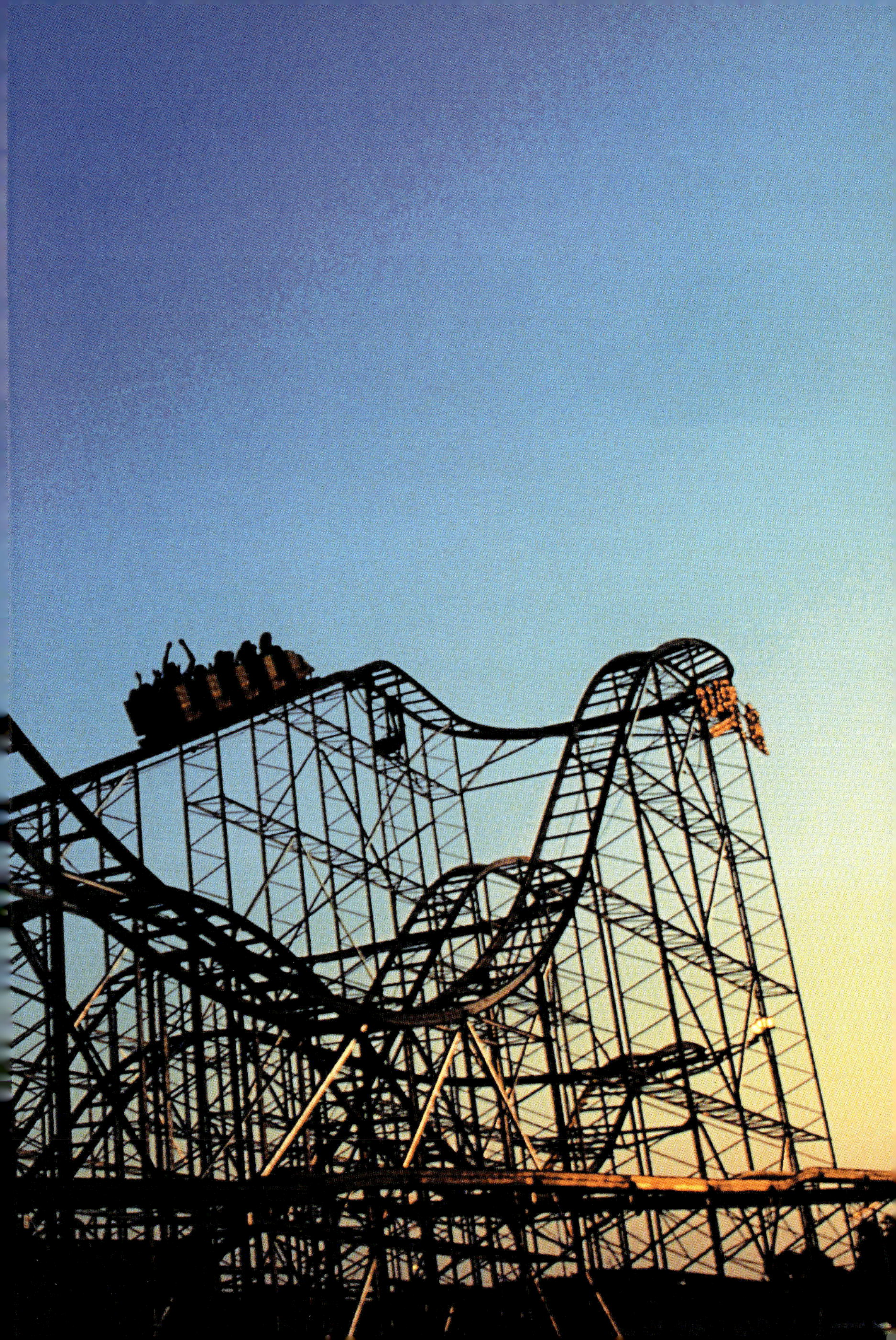

Here are some words about speed.

Slow

Fast

Slower   Faster

Slowest

Fastest

Speed up

Slow down

22

Are these things fast or slow?

Ride

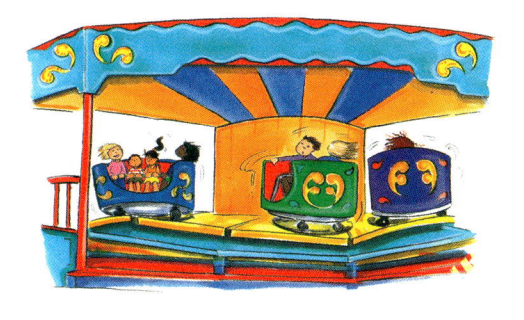

Car

Rocket

Bicycle

Rollercoaster

Can you write a story with these words?

23

Do you know?

A watch times how fast we can run.

A dial tells us how fast a car is going.

Signs tell people not to drive too fast.

24